Office, Juvenile Instructor

Heroines of Mormondom

Office, Juvenile Instructor

Heroines of Mormondom

ISBN/EAN: 9783337192624

Printed in Europe, USA, Canada, Australia, Japan

Cover: Foto ©Andreas Hilbeck / pixelio.de

More available books at **www.hansebooks.com**

HEROINES OF

"MORMONDOM,"

THE SECOND BOOK OF THE

NOBLE WOMEN'S LIVES SERIES.

SALT LAKE CITY, UTAH.

PUBLISHED AT THE JUVENILE INSTRUCTOR OFFICE.

1884.

PREFACE.

It affords us much pleasure to be able to present a second book of the "Noble Women's Lives Series" to the public. It will, we feel confident, prove no less interesting than its predecessor, and the lessons conveyed by the articles herein contained will doubtless be as instructive to its readers as any ever given.

The remarkable events here recorded are worthy of perusal and remembrance by all the youth among this people, as they will tend to strengthen faith in and love for the gospel for which noble men and women have suffered so much. The names, too, of such heroines as these, the sketches of whose lives we herewith give, should be held in honorable remembrance among this people, for no age or nation can present us with more illustrious examples of female faith, heroism and devotion.

We trust that this little work may find its way in the homes of all the Saints and prove a blessing to all who scan its pages. This is the earnest desire of

THE PUBLISHERS.

CONTENTS.

A NOBLE WOMAN'S EXPERIENCE.

A REMARKABLE LIFE.

A HEROINE OF HAUN'S MILL MASSACRE.

A NOBLE WOMAN'S EXPERIENCE.

CHAPTER I.

HYRUM SMITH, the Patriarch, married Jerusha Barden, November 2, 1826. They had six children, viz: Lovina, Mary, John, Hyrum, Jerusha and Sarah. Mary died when very young, and her mother died soon after the birth of her daughter, Sarah. Hyrum, the second son, died in Nauvoo, in 1842, aged eight years. The Patriarch married his second wife, Mary Fielding, in the year 1837, she entering upon the important duty of step-mother to five children, which task she performed, under the most trying and afflictive circumstances, with unwavering fidelity. She had two children, Joseph and Martha. Thus, you see, Hyrum Smith, the Patriarch of the Church of Jesus Christ of Latter-day Saints, was really a polygamist many years before the revelation on celestial marriage was written, though, perhaps, about the time it was given to the Prophet Joseph Smith; but not exactly in the sense in which the word is generally used, for both his wives were not living together on the

earth; still they were both alive, for the spirit never dies, and they were both his wives—the mothers
of his children. Marriage is ordained of God, and
when performed by the authority of His Priesthood, is an ordinance of the everlasting gospel,
and is not, therefore, merely a legal contract, but
pertains to time and all eternity to come, therefore
it is written in the Bible, "What God hath joined
together let no man put asunder."

There are a great many men who feel very bitter against the Latter-day Saints, and especially
against the doctrine of plural marriage, who have
married one or more wives after the death of their
first, that, had their marriages been solemnized in
the manner God has prescribed and by His authority, they themselves would be polygamists, for they,
as we, firmly believe in the immortality of the
soul, professing to be Christians and looking forward to the time when they will meet, in the
spirit world, their *wives* and the loved ones that
are dead. We can imagine the awkward situation
of a man, not believing in polygamy, meeting two
or more wives, with their children, in the spirit
world, each of them claiming him as husband and
father. "But," says one, "how will it be with a
woman who marries another husband after the
death of her first?" She will be the wife of the
one to whom she was married for time and eternity. But if God did not "join them together,"
and they were only married by mutual consent
until death parted them, their contract, or part-
nership ends with death, and there remains but

one way for those who died without the knowledge of the gospel to be united together for eternity. That is, for their living relatives or friends to attend to the ordinances of the gospel for them. "For, in the resurrection, they neither marry nor are given in marriage;" therefore marriage ordinances must be attended to here in the flesh. Hyrum Smith, however, was a polygamist before his death, he having had several women sealed to him by his brother, Joseph, some of whom are now living.

At the death of the Patriarch, June 27th, 1844, the care of the family fell upon his widow, Mary Smith. Besides the children there were two old ladies named respectively, Hannah Grinnels, who had been in the family many years, and Margaret Brysen. There was also a younger one, named Jane Wilson, who was troubled with fits and otherwise afflicted, and was, therefore, very dependent, and an old man, named George Mills, who had also been in the family eleven years, and was almost entirely blind and very crabbed. These and others, some of whom had been taken care of by the Patriarch out of charity, were members of the family and remained with them until after they arrived in the valley. "Old George," as he was sometimes called, had been a soldier in the British army, had never learned to read or write, and often acted upon impulse more than from the promptings of reason, which made it difficult, sometimes, to get along with him; but because he had been in the family so long—through the troubles of Missouri and Illinois—and had lost his eye-sight from the effects of brain fever and inflammation, caused by taking cold while in the pineries getting out timbers for the temple at Nauvoo, Widow Smith bore patiently all his peculiarities up to the time of her death. Besides those I have mentioned, Mercy R. Thompson, sister to Widow Smith, and her daughter, and Elder James Lawson were also members of the family.

On or about the 8th of September, 1846, the family, with others, were driven out of Nauvoo by the threats of the mob, and encamped on the banks of the Mississippi River, just below Montrose. There they were compelled to remain two or three days, in view of their comfortable homes just across the river, unable to travel for the want of teams, while the men were preparing to defend the city against the attack of the mob. They were thus under the necessity of witnessing the commencement of the memorable "Battle of Nauvoo;" but, before the cannonading ceased, they succeeded in moving out a few miles, away from the dreadful sound of it, where they remained until they obtained, by the change of property at a great sacrifice, teams and an outfit for the journey through Iowa to the Winter Quarters of the Saints, now Florence, Nebraska. Arriving at that point late in the Fall, they were obliged to turn out their work animals to pick their living through the Winter, during which some of their cattle, and eleven out of their thirteen horses died, leaving them very destitute of teams in the Spring.

In the Fall of 1847, Widow Smith and her brother, Joseph Fielding, made a trip into Missouri, with two teams, to purchase provisions for the family. Joseph, her son, accompanied them as teamster; he was then nine years of age. The team he drove consisted of two yokes of oxen, one yoke being young and only partially broke, which, with the fact that the roads were very bad with the Fall rains, full of stumps in places, sometimes hilly, and that he drove to St. Joseph, Missouri, and back, a distance of about three hundred miles, without meeting with one serious accident, proves that he must have been a fair teamster for a boy at his age.

At St. Joseph they purchased corn and other necessaries, getting their corn ground at Savannah, on their return journey. Wheat flour was a luxury beyond their reach, and one seldom enjoyed by many of the Latter-day Saints in those days. On their journey homeward they camped one evening at the edge of a small prairie, or open flat, surrounded by woods, where a large herd of cattle, on their way to market, was being pastured for the night, and turned out their teams, as usual, to graze. In the morning their best yoke of cattle was missing, at which they were greatly surprised, this being the first time their cattle had separated. Brother Fielding and Joseph at once started in search, over the prairie, through the tall, wet grass, in the woods, far and near, until they were almost exhausted with fatigue and hunger, and saturated to the skin; but their search was vain. Joseph returned first to the wagons, towards mid-day, and found his mother engaged in prayer. Brother Fielding arrived soon after, and they sat down to breakfast, which had long been waiting. ·

"Now," said Widow Smith, "while you are eating I will go down towards the river and see if I can find the cattle."

Brother Fielding remarked, "I think it is useless for you to start out to hunt the cattle; I have inquired of all the herdsmen and at every house for miles, and I believe they have been driven off." Joseph was evidently of the same opinion, still he had more faith in his mother finding them, if they could be found, than he had either in his uncle or himself. He knew that she had been praying to the Lord for assistance, and he felt almost sure that the Lord would hear her prayers. Doubtless he would have felt quite sure had he not been so disheartened by the apparently thorough but fruitless search of the morning. He felt, however to follow her example: he prayed that his mother might be guided to the cattle, and exercised all the faith he could muster, striving hard to feel confident that she would be successful. As she was following the little stream, directly in the course she had taken on leaving the wagons, one of the drovers rode up on the opposite side and said, "Madam, I saw your cattle this morning over in those woods," pointing almost directly opposite to the course she was taking. She paid no attention to him, but passed right on. He repeated his information; still she did not heed him. He then rode off hurriedly, and, in a few moments, with his companions, began to gather up their cattle and start them on the road towards St. Joseph. She had not gone far when she came upon a small ravine filled with tall willows and brush; but not tall enough to be seen above the high grass of the prairie. In a dense cluster of these willows she found the oxen so entangled in the brush, and fastened by means of withes, that it was with great difficulty that she extricated them from their entanglement. This was evidently the work of these honest (?) drovers, who so hurriedly disappeared —seeing they could not turn her from her course —perhaps in search of estray honesty, which it is to be hoped they found.

This circumstance made an indelible impression upon the mind of the lad, Joseph. He had witnessed many evidences of God's mercy, in answer to prayer, before; but none that seemed to strike him so forcibly as this. Young as he was, he realized his mother's anxiety to emigrate with her family to the valley in the Spring, and their dependence upon their teams to perform that journey, which, to him, seemed a formidable, if not an impossible, undertaking in their impoverished circumstances. It was this that made him so disheartened and sorrowful when he feared that the cattle would never be found. Besides, it seemed to him that he could not bear to see such a loss and disappointment come upon his mother, whose life he had known, from his earliest recollection, had been a life of toil and struggle for the main-

tenance and welfare of her family.   His joy, therefore, as he looked through tears of gratitude to God
for His kind mercy extended to the "widow and
the fatherless" may be imagined, as he ran to meet
his mother driving the oxen towards the wagons.

CHAPTER II.

JOSEPH was herd-boy.   One bright morning
sometime in the Fall of 1847, in company with his
herd-boy companions, whose names were Alden
Burdick, (almost a young man, and very sober and
steady), Thomas Burdick, cousin to Alden, about
Joseph's size, but somewhat older, and Isaac Block-
some, younger, he started out with his cattle as
usual for the herd grounds, some two miles from
Winter Quarters.   They had two horses, both
belonging to the Burdicks, and a pet jack belonging
to Joseph.   Their herd that day comprised not
only the cows and young stock, but the work oxen,
which for some cause were unemployed.

Alden proposed to take a trip on foot through
the hazel, and gather nuts for the party, and by
the "lower road" meet the boys at the spring on
the herd ground, while they drove the herd by the
"upper road" which was free from brush.   This
arrangement just suited Joseph and Thomas, for
they were very fond of a little sport, and his
absence would afford them full scope; while his
presence served as an extinguisher upon the exu-
berance of their mirth.   Joseph rode Alden's bay

mare, a very fine animal; Thomas, his father's
black pony, and Isaac the pet Jack.   This Jack
had deformed or crooked fore-legs, and was very
knowing in his way; so "Ike" and the Jack were
the subjects chosen by Joseph and Thomas for
their sport.   They would tickle "Jackie," and
plague him, he would kick up, stick his head down,
hump up his back and run, while Isaac struggled
in vain to guide or hold him by the bridle reins,
for like the rest of his tribe he was very headstrong
when abused.   No harm or even offense to Isaac
was intended; but they carried their fun too far;
Isaac was offended, and returned home on foot,
turning loose the Jack with the bridle on.   We
will not try to excuse Joseph and Thomas in this
rudeness to Isaac, for although they were well-
meaning boys, it was no doubt very wrong to carry
their frolics so far as to offend or hurt the feelings
of their playmate, and especially as he was
younger than they; but in justice to them it is fair
to say they were heartily sorry when they found
they had given such sore offense.

When Joseph and Thomas arrived at the spring
they set down their dinner pails by it, mounted
their horses again, and began to amuse themselves
by running short races, jumping ditches and riding
about.   They would not have done this had Alden
been there.   They had not even done such a thing
before, although the same opportunity had not
been wanting; but for some reason—ever fond of
frolic and mischief—they were more than usually
so this morning.   It is said that not even a "spar-

row falls to the ground" without God's notice, is it unreasonable to suppose that He saw these boys? And as He overrules the actions of even the wicked, and causes their "wrath to praise Him;" would it be inconsistent to suppose that the Lord overruled the frolics of these mischievous, but not wicked boys on this occasion for good, perhaps for their deliverance and salvation? We shall see.

While they were riding about and the cattle were feeding down the little spring creek toward a point of the hill that jutted out into the little valley about half a mile distant, the "leaders" being about half way to it, a gang of Indians on horseback, painted, their hair daubed with white clay, stripped to the skin, suddenly appeared from behind the hill, whooping and charging at full speed toward them. Now, had these boys turned out their horses, as under other circumstances they should, and no doubt would, have done, they and the cattle would have been an easy prey to the Indians, the boys themselves being completely at their mercy, such mercy, as might be expected from a thieving band of savages. In an instant, Thomas put his pony under full run for home, crying at the top of his voice, "Indians, Indians!" At the same instant Joseph set out at full speed for the head of the herd, with a view to save them if possible.

He only could tell the multitude of his thoughts in that single moment. Boy as he was, he made a desperate resolve. His mother, his brother and sisters and their dependence upon their cattle for transportation to the Valley in the Spring, occupied his thoughts and nerved him to meet the Indians half-way, and risk his life to save the cattle from being driven off by them. At the moment that he reached the foremost of the herd, the Indians, with terrific yells reached the same spot, which frightened the cattle so, that with the almost superhuman effort of the little boy to head them in the right direction, and at the same time to elude the grasp of the Indians, in an instant they were all on the stampede towards home. Here the Indians divided, the foremost passing by Joseph in hot pursuit of Thomas, who by this time had reached the brow of the hill on the upper road leading to town, but he was on foot. He had left his pony, knowing the Indians could outrun—and perhaps would overtake him. And thinking they would be satisfied with only the horse, and by leaving that he could make good his escape.

Joseph's horse was fleeter on foot, besides, he was determined to sell what he had to, at the dearest possible rate. The rest of the Indians of the first gang, about half a dozen, endeavored to capture him; but in a miraculous manner he eluded them contriving to keep the cattle headed in the direction of the lower road towards home, until he reached the head of the spring. Here the Indians who pursued Thomas—excepting the one in possession of Thomas' horse, which he had captured and was leading away towards the point— met him, turning his horse around the spring and down the course of the stream, the whole gang of

Indians in full chase. He could outrun them, and
had he now, freed from the herd, been in the direction of home he could have made his escape; but
as he reached a point opposite the hill from whence
the Indians came, he was met by another gang
who had crossed the stream for that purpose; again
turning his horse. Making a circuit, he once
more got started towards home. His faithful
animal began to lose breath and flag. He could
still, however, keep out of the reach of his pursuers;
but now the hindmost in the down race began to
file in before him, as he had turned about, by
forming a platoon and veering to the right or left
in front, as he endeavored to pass, they obstructed
his course, so that those behind overtook him just
as he once more reached the spring. Riding up
on either side, one Indian fiercely took him by the
right arm, another by the left leg, while a third
was prepared to close in and secure his horse.
Having forced his reins from his grip, they raised
him from the saddle, slackened speed till his horse
ran from under him, then dashed him to the ground
among their horses' feet while running at great
speed. He was considerably stunned by the fall,
but fortunately escaped further injury, notwith-
standing, perhaps a dozen horses passed over him.
As he rose to his feet, several men were in sight
on the top of the hill, with pitchforks in their
hands at the sight of whom the Indians fled in the
direction they had come. These men had been
alarmed by Thomas' cry of Indians, while on their
way to the hay fields, and reached the place in

time to see Joseph's horse captured and another incident which was rather amusing. The Jack, which did not stampede with the cattle, had strayed off alone toward the point of the hill, still wearing his bridle. An old Indian with some corn in a buckskin sack was trying to catch him; but "Jackie" did not fancy Mr. Indian, although not afraid of him, and so would wheel from him as he would attempt to take hold of the bridle. As the men appeared, the Indian made a desperate lunge to catch the Jack, but was kicked over, and his corn spilt on the ground. The Indian jumped up and took to his heels, and "Jackie" deliberately ate up his corn. By this time the cattle were scattered off in the brush lining the lower road, still heading towards town. The men with the pitchforks soon disappeared from the hill, continuing on to the hay-fields, and Joseph found himself alone, affording him a good opportunity to reflect on his escape and situation. The truth is, his own thoughts made him more afraid than did the Indians. What if they should return to complete their task, which he had been instrumental in so signally defeating? They would evidently show him no mercy. They had tried to trample him to death with their horses, and what could he do on foot and alone? It would take him a long time to gather up the cattle, from among the brush. The Indians might return any moment, there was nothing to prevent them doing so. These were his thoughts; he concluded therefore that time was precious, and that he would follow the example, now, of Thomas, and "make tracks" for home. When he arrived the people had gathered in the old bowery, and were busy organizing two companies, one of foot and the other of horsemen, to pursue the Indians. All was excitement, his mother and the family were almost distracted, supposing he had been killed or captured by the Indians. Thomas had told the whole story so far as he knew it, the supposition was therefore inevitable; judge, therefore, of the happy surprise of his mother and sisters on seeing him, not only alive, but uninjured. Their tears of joy were even more copious than those of grief a moment before.

But Joseph's sorrow had not yet began. He and Thomas returned with the company of armed men on foot to hunt for the cattle, while the horsemen were to pursue the Indians, if possible, to recover the horses. When they arrived again at the spring no sign of the cattle could be seen; even the dinner pails had been taken away. On looking around, the saddle blanket from the horse Joseph rode was found near the spring. Was this evidence that the Indians had returned as Joseph had suspected? And had they, after all, succeeded in driving off the cattle? These were the questions which arose. All that day did they hunt, but in vain, to find any further trace of them; and as they finally gave up the search and bent their weary steps towards home, all hope of success seemingly fled. Joseph could no longer suppress the heavy weight of grief that filled his heart, and he gave vent to it in bitter tears, and wished he had been a man.

It is said, "calms succeed storms," "and one ex-treme follows another," etc.   Certainly joy followed closely on the heels of grief more than once this day, for when Joseph and Thomas reached home, to their surprise and unspeakable joy, they found all their cattle safely corraled in their yards where they had been all the afternoon.   Alden, it seems, reached the herd ground just after Joseph had left. He found the cattle straying off in the wrong direction unherded, and he could find no trace of the boys or horses, although he discovered the dinner pails at the spring as usual.   When he had thoroughly satisfied himself by observations that all was not right, and perhaps something very serious was the matter, he came to the conclusion to take the dinner pails, gather up the cattle and go home, which he did by the lower road, reaching home some time after the company had left by the upper road in search of them.   He of course learned the particulars of the whole affair, and must have felt thankful that he had escaped.   A messenger was sent to notify the company of the safety of the cattle, but for some reason he did not overtake them.

In the Spring of 1847, George Mills was fitted out with a team and went in the company of Pres-ident Young as one of the Pioneers to the Valley; and soon, a portion of the family in the care of Brother James Lawson, emigrated from "Winter Quarters," arriving in the Valley that Fall.

In the Spring of 1848, a tremendous effort was made by the Saints to emigrate to the Valley on

a grand scale.   No one was more anxious than
Widow Smith; but to accomplish it seemed an
impossibility.   She still had a large and comparatively helpless family.   Her two sons, John and
Joseph, mere boys, being her only support; the
men folks, as they were called, Brothers J. Lawson
and G. Mills being in the Valley with the teams
they had taken.   Without teams sufficient to draw
the number of wagons necessary to haul provisions
and outfit for the family, and without means to
purchase, or friends who were in circumstances to
assist, she determined to make the attempt, and
trust in the Lord for the issue.   Accordingly every
nerve was strained, and every available object
was brought into requisition.   "Jackie" was traded
off for provisions; cows and calves were yoked
up, two wagons lashed together, and team barely
sufficient to draw one was hitched on to them, and
in this manner they rolled out from Winter Quarters some time in May.   After a series of the most
amusing aud trying circumstances, such as stick-
ing in the mud, doubling teams up all the little
hills and crashing at ungovernable speed down
the opposite sides, breaking wagon tongues and
reaches, upsetting, and vainly endeavoring to
control wild steers, heifers and unbroken cows,
they finally succeeded in reaching the Elk Horn,
where the companies were being organized for the
plains.

Here, Widow Smith reported herself to President
Kimball, as having "started for the Valley." Meantime, she had left no stone unturned or problem

untried, which promised assistance in effecting
the necessary of preparations for the journey. She
had done to her utmost, and still the way looked
dark and impossible.

President Kimball consigned her to Captain
———'s fifty. The captain was present; said he,
"Widow Smith, how many wagons have you?"
"Seven."
"How many yokes of oxen have you?"
"Four," and so many cows and calves.
"Well," says the captain, "Widow Smith, it is
folly for you to start in this manner; you never
can make the journey, and if you try it, you will be
a burden upon the company the whole way. My
advice to you is, go back to Winter Quarters and
wait till you can get help."

This speech aroused the indignation of Joseph,
who stood by and heard it; he thought it was poor
consolation to his mother who was struggling so
hard, even against hope as it were, for her deliverance; and if he had been a little older it is possible that he would have said some very harsh
things to the captain; but as it was, he busied
himself with his thoughts and bit his lips.

Widow Smith calmly replied, "Father———"
(he was an aged man,) "I will beat you to the
Valley and will ask no help from you either!"

This seemed to nettle the old gentleman, for he
was high metal. It is possible that he never forgot
this prediction, and that it influenced his conduct
towards her more or less from that time forth as
long as he lived, and especially during the journey.

1*

While the companies were lying at Elk Horn, Widow Smith sent back to Winter Quarters, and by the blessing of God, succeeded in buying on credit, and hiring for the journey, several yokes of oxen from brethren who were not able to emigrate that year, (among these brethren one Brother Rogers was ever gratefully remembered by the family). When the companies were ready to start, Widow Smith and her family were somewhat better prepared for the journey and rolled out with lighter hearts and better prospects than favored their egress from Winter Quarters. But Joseph often wished that his mother had been consigned to some other company, for although everything seemed to move along pleasantly, his ears were frequently saluted with expressions which seemed to be prompted by feelings of disappointment and regret at his mother's prosperity and success— expressions which, it seemed to him, were made expressly for his ear. To this, however, he paid as little regard as it was possible for a boy of his temperament to do. One cause for annoyance was the fact that his mother would not permit him to stand guard at nights the same as a man or his older brother John, when the Captain required it. She was willing for him to herd in the day time and do his duty in everything that seemed to her in reason could be required of him; but, as he was only ten years of age, she did not consider him old enough to do guard duty at nights to protect the camp from Indians, stampedes, etc., therefore, when the captain required him to stand guard,

Widow Smith objected. He was, therefore, frequently sneered at as being "petted by his mother," which was a sore trial to him.

CHAPTER III.

ONE day the company overtook President Kimball's company, which was traveling ahead of them; this was somewhere near the north fork of the Platte River. Jane Wilson, who has been mentioned as being a member of the family of Widow Smith, and as being troubled with fits, etc., and withal very fond of snuff, started ahead to overtake her mother, who was in the family of Bishop N. K. Whitney, in President Kimball's company, supposing both companies would camp together, and she could easily return to her own camp in the evening. But, early in the afternoon, our captain ordered a halt, and camped for that night and the next day. This move, unfortunately, compelled poor Jane to continue on with her mother in the preceding company.

Towards evening the captain took a position in the center of the corral formed by the wagons, and called the company together, and then cried out:

"Is all right in the camp? Is all right in the camp?"

Not supposing for a moment that anything was wrong, no one replied. He repeated the question again and again, each time increasing his vehemence, until some began to feel alarmed. Old "Uncle Tommie" Harrington replied in good English style, "Nout's the matter wi me; nout's the matter wi me;" and one after another replied, "Nothing is the matter with me," until it came to Widow Smith, at which, in a towering rage, the captain exclaimed, "All's right in the camp, and a poor woman lost!"

Widow Smith replied, "She is not lost; she is with her mother, and as safe as I am."

At which the captain lost all control of his temper, and fairly screamed out, "I rebuke you, Widow Smith, in the name of the Lord!" pouring forth a tirade of abuse upon her. Nothing would pacify him till she proposed to send her son John ahead to find Jane. It was almost dark, and he would doubtless have to travel until nearly midnight before he would overtake the company; but he started, alone and unarmed, in an unknown region, an Indian country, infested by hordes of hungry wolves, ravenous for the dead cattle strewn here and there along the road, which drew them in such numbers that their howlings awakened the echoes of the night, making it hideous and disturbing the slumbers of the camps.

That night was spent by Widow Smith in prayer and anguish for the safety of her son; but the next day John returned all safe, and reported that he had found Jane all right with her mother. Widow Smith's fears for his safety, although perhaps unnecessary, were not groundless, as his account of his night's trip proved. The wolves growled and glared at him as he passed along, not caring even to get out of the road for him; their eyes gleaming like balls of fire through the darkness on every hand; but they did not molest him; still, the task was one that would have made a timid person shudder and shrink from its performance.

Another circumstance occurred, while camped at this place, which had a wonderful influence, some time afterwards, upon Captain ——'s mind. There was a party of the brethren started out on a hunting expedition for the day. A boy, that was driving team for Widow Smith, but little larger than Joseph, although several years his senior, accompanied them, riding with the captain in his carriage, which they took along to carry their game in. This boy (he is now a man, and no doubt a good Latter-day Saint) was a very great favorite of the captain's; and was often cited by him as a worthy example for Joseph, as he stood guard, and was very obliging and obedient to him. During the day the captain left him in charge of his carriage and team, while he went some distance away in search of game, charging W—— not to leave the spot until he returned. Soon after the captain got out of sight, W—— drove off in pursuit of some of the brethren in another direction, and when he overtook them, strange to say, he told a most foolish and flimsy story, which aroused their suspicion. They charged him with falsehood, but he unwisely stuck to his story. It was this: "Captain —— had sent him to tell them to drive the game down to a certain point, so that he (the captain) might have a shot as well as they." Having done this he started back to his post, expecting to get there, of course, before the captain returned. But unfortunately for his good reputation with the captain, he was too late. The captain had returned, but the carriage was gone, not knowing the reason he doubtless became alarmed, as he immediately started in search, instead of waiting to see if it would return. He missed connection, and was subjected to a tedious tramp and great anxiety, until he fell in with those brethren, who related the strange interview they had had with W——— and the mystery was explained. Returning again, there he found the carriage and W——— all right, looking innocent and dutiful, little suspecting that the captain knew all, and the storm that was about to burst upon his devoted head. But like a thunder-clap the storm came. At first W——— affected bewilderment, putting on an air of injured innocence, but soon gave way before the avalanche of wrath hurled upon him. Poor fellow! he had destroyed the captain's confidence in him, and would he ever regain it? The reader can readily imagine this would be a difficult matter. Sometime after this, the captain went out from camp with his carriage to gather saleratus, and on the way overtook Joseph on foot. To Joseph's utter astonishment, the captain stopped and invited him to ride. There was another brother in the carriage with him. As they went along the captain told this story, and concluded by saying, "Now, Joseph, since W——— has betrayed my confidence so that I dare not trust him any more, you shall take his place. I don't believe you will deceive me." Joseph, in the best manner he possibly could, declined the honor proffered to him.

Passing over from the Platte to the Sweetwater, the cattle suffered extremely from the heat, the drought, and the scarcity of feed, being compelled to browse on dry rabbit brush, sage brush, weeds and such feed as they could find, all of which had been well picked over by the preceding companies. Captain ———'s company being one of the last, still keeping along, frequently in sight of, and sometimes camping with President Kimball's company which was very large. One day as they were moving along slowly through the hot sand and dust, the sun pouring down with excessive heat, toward noon one of Widow Smith's best oxen laid down in the yoke, rolled over on his side, and stiffened out his legs spasmodically, evidently in the throes of death. The unanimous opinion was that he was poisoned. All the hindmost teams of course stopped, the people coming forward to know what was the matter. In a short time the captain, who was in advance of the company, perceiving that something was wrong, came to the spot.

Perhaps no one supposed for a moment that the ox would ever recover. The captain's first words on seeing him, were:

"He is dead, there is no use working with him; we'll have to fix up some way to take the Widow along, I told her she would be a burden upon the company."

Meantime Widow Smith had been searching for a bottle of consecrated oil in one of the wagons, and now came forward with it, and asked her brother, Joseph Fielding, and the other brethren, to administer to the ox, thinking the Lord would raise him up. They did so, pouring a portion of the oil on the top of his head, between and back of the horns, and all laid hands upon him, and one prayed, administering the ordinance as they would have done to a human being that was sick. Can you guess the result? In a moment he gathered his legs under him, and at the first word arose to his feet, and traveled right off as well as ever. He was not even unyoked from his mate. The captain, it may well be supposed, now heartily regretted his hasty conclusions and unhappy expressions. They had not gone very far when another and exactly similar circumstance occurred. This time also it was one of her best oxen, the loss of either would have effectually crippled one team, as they had no cattle to spare. But the Lord mercifully heard their prayers, and recognized the holy ordinance of anointing and prayer, and the authority of the Priesthood when applied in behalf of even a poor dumb brute! Sincere gratitude from more than one heart in that family, went up unto the Lord that day for His visible interposition in their behalf. At or near a place called Rattlesnake Bend, on the Sweetwater, one of Widow Smith's oxen died of sheer old age, and consequent poverty. He had been comparatively useless for some time, merely carrying his end of the yoke without being of any further service in the team; he was therefore no great loss.

At the last crossing of the Sweetwater, Widow Smith was met by James Lawson, with a span of horses and a wagon, from the Valley. This enabled her to unload one wagon, and send it, with the best team, back to Winter Quarters to assist another family the next season. Elder Joel Terry returned with the team. At this place the captain was very unfortunate; several of his best cattle and a valuable mule laid down and died, supposed to have been caused by eating poisonous weeds. There was no one in the camp who did not feel a lively sympathy for the Captain, he took it to heart very much. He was under the necessity of obtaining help, and Widow Smith was the first to offer it to him, but he refused to accept of it from her hands. Joseph sympathized with him, and would gladly have done anything in his power to aid him; but here again, it is painful to say, he repulsed his sympathy and chilled his heart and feelings more and more by insinuating to others, in his presence, that Widow Smith had poisoned his cattle! Saying, "Why should my cattle, and nobody's else, die in this manner? There is more than a chance about this. It was well planned," etc., expressly for his ear. This last thrust was the severing blow. Joseph resolved, some day, to demand satisfaction not only for this, but for every other indignity he had heaped upon his mother.

On the 22nd of September, 1848, Captain————'s
fifty crossed over the "Big Mountain," when they
had the first glimpse of Salt Lake Valley.   It was
a beautiful day.   Fleecy clouds hung round over
the summits of the highest mountains, casting
their shadows down the valley beneath, hightening,
by contrast, the golden hue of the sun's rays which
fell through the openings upon the dry bunch-
grass and sage-bush plains, gilding them with
fairy brightness, and making the arid desert to
seem like an enchanted spot.   Every heart rejoiced
and with lingering fondness, wistfully gazed from
the summit of the mountain upon the western side
of the valley revealed to view—the goal of their
wearisome journey.   The ascent from the east was
gradual, but long and fatiguing for the teams; it
was in the afternoon, therefore, when they reached
the top.   The descent to the west was far more
precipitous and abrupt.   They were obliged to
rough-lock the hind wheels of the wagons, and, as
they were not needed, the forward cattle were
turned loose to be driven to the foot of the mountain or to camp, the "wheelers" only being retained
on the wagons.   Desirous of shortening the next
day's journey as much as possible—as that was to
bring them into the Valley—they drove on till a
late hour in the night, over very rough roads
much of the way, and skirted with oak brush and
groves of trees.   They finally camped near the
eastern foot of the "Little Mountain."   During
this night's drive several of Widow Smith's cows—
that had been turned loose from the teams—were

lost in the brush. Early next morning John returned on horseback to hunt for them, their service in the teams being necessary to proceed.

At an earlier hour than usual the Captain gave orders for the company to start—knowing well the circumstances of the Widow, and that she would be obliged to remain till John returned with the lost cattle—accordingly the company rolled out, leaving her and her family alone.

It was fortunate that Brother James Lawson was with them, for he knew the road, and if necessary, could pilot them down the canyon in the night. Joseph thought of his mother's prediction at Elk Horn, and so did the Captain, and he was determined that he would win this point, although he had lost all the others, and prove her prediction false. "I will beat you to the Valley, and ask no help from you either," rang in Joseph's ears; he could not reconcile these words with possibility, though he knew his mother always told the truth, but how could this come true? Hours, to him, seemed like days as they waited, hour after hour, for John to return. All this time the company was slowly tugging away up the mountain, lifting at the wheels, geeing and hawing, twisting along a few steps, then blocking the wheels for the cattle to rest and take breath, now doubling a team, and now a crowd rushing to stop a wagon, too heavy for the exhausted team, and prevent its rolling backward down the hill, dragging the cattle along with it. While in this condition, to heighten the distress and balk the teams, a cloud, as it were, burst over their heads, sending down the rain in torrents, as it seldom rains in this country, throwing the company into utter confusion. The cattle refused to pull, would not face the beating storm, and to save the wagons from crashing down the mountain, upsetting, etc., they were obliged to unhitch them, and block. all the wheels. While the teamsters sought shelter, the storm drove the cattle in every direction through the brush and into the ravines, and into every nook they could find, so that when it subsided it was a day's work to find them, and get them together. Meantime Widow Smith's cattle—except those lost—were tied to the wagons, and were safe. In a few moments after the storm, John brought up those which had been lost, and they hitched up, making as early a start as they usually did in the mornings, rolled up the mountain, passing the company in their confused situation, and feeling that every tie had been sundered that bound them to the captain, continued on to the Valley, and arrived at "Old Fort," about ten o'clock on the night of the 23rd of September, all well and thankful. The next morning was Sabbath, the whole family went to the bowery to meeting. Presidents Young and Kimball preached. This was the first time that Joseph had ever heard them, to his recollection, in public; and he exclaimed to himself: "These are the men of God, who are gathering the Saints to the Valley." This was a meeting long to be remembered by those present. President Young spoke as though he felt: "Now, God's people are free," and the way of their deliverance had been wrought out. That evening Captain————and his company arrived, dusty and weary, too late for the excellent meetings and the day of sweet rest enjoyed by the Widow and her family. Once more, in silver tones, rang through Joseph's ears. "Father————, I will beat you to the Valley, and will ask no help from you either!" ·   J. F. S.

A REMARKABLE LIFE.

BY "HOMESPUN."

CHAPTER I.

MANY of the noblest lives have been lived in obscurity and in poverty. Nobility and virtue are never dependent upon surroundings. And when you have read the simple little chronicle which I am about to relate, I think you will agree with me that even though humble and retiring, the subject of this sketch was one of nature's own heroines.

In a little cottage in Bravon, Lees-Mersem, England, lived an old lady named Harris. She was given to study although very meagrely educated. She was feeble and sat a great deal of her time poring over her Bible.

One day her granddaughter came to visit her, bringing her little daughter, Mary, with her. The old lady had been reading her Bible, and as her daughter came in she said:

"My dear, I have been reading some of the great prophecies concerning the last days, and I feel sure that either you or yours will live to see many of them fulfilled."

"Not so, grandmother," answered the woman, whose name was Mrs. Dunster, "thou wast always visionary; put by such thoughts. Our religion's good enough for the like of us."

The old lady arose, unheeding her granddaughter's warm reply, and placing her hands on the little girl's head, said solemnly:

"Here's Mary; she shall grow up and wander away from you all and break her bread in different nations."

The solemnity of her great-grandmother's manner and the peculiar spirit that accompanied the words made a vivid impression on the little girl's mind. How well that strange prophecy has been fulfilled you and I, my reader, can tell hereafter.

The little girl, whose name was Mary Dunster, and who was born in Lympne, Kent, December 26, 1818, grew up and when sixteen years of age was asked in marriage by William Chittenden, who was a laborer on an adjoining farm. She did not feel very willing, but the young man urged her so warmly that she hesitated before refusing him. She had always had an irresistible desire to go to

America, where many emigrants were then going from England.

At last she consented to be his wife on one condition: that he would take her to America. Very bravely promised the lover, but not until forty-two years afterwards did he fulfill that promise.

After they were married they settled down to work and lived, William as farm laborer, in Lympne for four years. Two children were born to them in this place, Mary Ann, born June, 15, 1836, and Henry, born August 18, 1838.

Four years after their marriage, at which time the introduction of convicts into Australia was prohibited and the government of England offered good inducement to skilled laborers to settle up the country, William Chittenden concluded to go to Australia. Previous to this time the English convicts, who were under life sentence, had been sent down to Australia, landing generally at Botany Bay. These convicts were brought down and sold as life slaves to those freeholders who were willing and able to purchase their labor. Sometimes they escaped from their masters and made their way into the interior of the country. These escaped convicts herded together in small parties or bands, and are called "bush-rangers." They have now become a powerful tribe, fierce, vindictive and unlawful. They resemble very nearly, in occupation and temperament, the wild Bedouins of Asia and the wild tribes of Arabs or Berbers of northern Africa.

Between the years of 1840 and 1850, England transported many skilled laborers and artizans to Australia to build up and colonize her possessions in the southern seas. Numbers of the husband's countrymen were going down to the "new country," and he resolved to go too. Mary objected; she wanted to go to America. I think, between you and me, that she used sometimes to remind her husband sharply of his unfulfilled promise. But his was a calm, kind, but essentially self-willed disposition, that listened good-naturedly to all Mary might and did say, but was no whit moved thereby to give up his own way. And so, after much controversy, the removal to Australia was decided upon and accomplished.

The young couple had determined to engage a farm on shares, and so went, immediately upon their arrival, to a country part near Botany Bay. Here they remained a short time and then went up to Camden, which is about one hundred miles from Sydney. William took a farm and then commenced a long career of farming in Australia. Most of their children were born there.

And now let me tell you something of the character of this same Mary, ere I relate to you two strange dreams which she had while living at Camden.

She was a medium-sized, well-built woman, with kind, gray eyes and a pleasant but firm mouth. Her step was quick, and her manner was full of warm-hearted simplicity. She it was who ruled the children, administering with firm justice the rod of correction. Her husband contented himself by controlling his wife, leaving the whole of the remainder of the domestic regimen entirely in her hands. She was never disobeyed by her children. But withal "father" was a tenderer name to their large flock of girls than was "mother." But with all her firmness, she was far too womanly to possess one grain of obstinacy. When it was her duty to yield she could do so gracefully. With these qualities Mary united a sound business capacity, economy, thrift and extreme cleanliness. She was, and always has been, a remarkably healthy woman. With these gifts she had something of the visionary or semi-prophetic character of her great-grandmother Harris.

She has been a dreamer, and her dreams have been of a prophetic character. Most of them require no interpretation, but are simple forecasts, as it were, of the future.

One dream, which was indelibly impressed upon her mind, occurred to her just before the birth of her eighth daughter, Elizabeth. It was as follows:

She dreamed she had to travel a long way. At last she reached a stately white building, with projecting buttresses and towers. Going up the broad steps she entered a room filled with beautiful books. Seeing a door ajar, she walked into the adjoining room. There sat twelve men around a large table, and each man held a pen. They were looking up as though awaiting some message from above. She drew back, so as not to attract attention, when a voice said distinctly to her: "You will have to come here to be married." The thought passed through her mind, "I *am* married and why, therefore, should I come here to be married?

She went on out of the building and walked through the streets of the city that were near the building. The streets were straight and clean, with little streams of water running down under the shade-trees that bordered the foot-paths. Everything was clean and beautiful to look upon. Footbridges spanned the little streams, and the houses were clean and comfortable. She saw just ahead of her a woman driving a cow, with whom she felt a desire to speak, but before she could reach her, the woman had gone in at one of the gates. She walked on, pleased with all she saw. Raising her eyes she saw in the distance, coming to the city, what looked like an immense flock of sheep. But as they came nearer she saw they were people, all clothed in white raiment. They passed by and went on to the white building. "Ah!" thought Mary, "if I was there now, that I might know what it all meant!" But she felt compelled to go the other way. And so the dream ended.

When she awoke she related the strange episode to her husband and told him she believed her coming confinement would prove fatal. She thought the beautiful place she had seen could only be in heaven, as she had never seen anything like it upon the earth. William comforted her, but the spirit of the dream never left her.

However her little babe was born and she resumed her household duties.

———◆━◆━◆———

CHAPTER II.

Two years passed away, and ere they are passed let us stop a moment and see a little of this new country which lies away on the opposite side of the earth from America.

Australia, as you may all see, my readers, by getting out your geographies, is in the Pacific Ocean, down in the tropics and lying south-east of Asia. It is generally called a continent; but it looks very small, does it not, compared to Asia or either of the Americas? Now, look down on the south-east coast of this little continent and you will see Botany Bay and the city of Sydney lying close together. Look a little to the south-west of Sydney and you will find Goulburn. Camden, which is a comparatively new town, is not marked on the old maps, lies between Sydney and Goulburn.

This region you will find marked as the "gold region." But gold was not discovered until 1857, eleven years after the Chiltendens settled in their new home.

The country in New South Wales is good for farming and grazing; with the exception that it is subject to extremes of drouth and floods. There are no high mountain ranges, and very few rivers. There is no snow there, and the Winter season is a rainy season instead of being cold and freezing like our Winters. There are trees in that country which shed their bark instead of their leaves. I shall speak of these trees and the uses to which their bark is put further on. Then, there grows a native cherry, which has the pit on the outside, and the fruit inside. Wouldn't that be queer?

There are many precious stones found in this country, and also considerable gold; but the discovery of gold failed to excite William Chittenden, or turn him from the even tenor of his way.

On the 15th of April, 1853, a son was born to the Chittendens, who was christened William John, but who only lived a few weeks.

Some time after his death Mary dreamed that she was lying in her bed asleep. It was, as you might say, a dream within a dream. As she lay sleeping two men, each carrying a satchel in one hand and a cane in the other, came to the foot of her bed. She dreamed then that she awoke from her dream and looked earnestly at these two men; so earnestly that their faces were indelibly fixed upon her memory. One of them held out to her a little book.

"What is the use of my taking the book?" she thought within herself, "I cannot read a line, for I have never learned to read." Then, after a moment's hesitation, she thought, "Why, I can take it and my children can read it to me." So she took the book.

One of the men said these remarkable words to her:

"We are clothed upon with power to preach to the people."

She awoke in reality then, with those strange words thrilling her with a new power she had never felt before. She roused her husband up and related her dream, and he replied kindly to her.

They had now been married eighteen years and Mary had borne seven girls and two boys; neither of the two boys, however, had lived but a short time. The farm upon which they lived had been rented, or leased, from a large land-owner named McArthur, for twenty-one years. This McArthur owned some thousands of acres of farming and grazing land in this region, which was leased in farms of various proportions. .

The Chittendens' farm consisted of two hundred acres, and was mostly farming land. The terms upon which they leased it were very similar to others in that country. For the first five years they paid sixpence an acre. After that it was ten shillings an acre.

William put up the house in which they lived, and an odd house it was, too. First he took a number of poles, or uprights, which he placed in the earth at regular distances. With these he made the framework of his house. Between these uprights were placed smaller poles. Then he took fine willows and wove them, or turned them round the center, or smaller pole, resting the ends on the larger poles. In and out went these willows, something the same way as you will see willow fences here.   Then he made a thick mud and well covered the whole, inside and out.   Next came a good plaster of lime and sand, and finally all was whitewashed.   The roof was made with rafters laid across the top.   Now came in this bark about which I told you.   Going up to the forests which were found on the near hillsides, the bark was cut in the lengths wanted at the top and bottom of the tree; then with a sharp knife split on two sides, upon which it peeled off in thick, straight slabs. It was then nailed on in the place of shingles, each one overlaping the under one.   Then the floor was nailed down with wooden pegs, "adzed" off and finally smoothed with a jack-plane.

In this manner one large sitting-room, two bedrooms, a dairy and a kitchen, detached from the main building, were built; to which was afterwards added a long porch to the front of the house, which faced east, the rooms all being built in a row.

Mary cooked upon a brick oven, which was built upon a little standard just between the kitchen and the house.

Large fire-places were built in the kitchen and sitting-room.   The one in the kitchen, being big enough to take three immense logs, which would burn steadily for a whole week.

The dairy was well furnished with pans, pails, etc.

CHAPTER III.

In 1853, William decided to take a trip up to Sydney to sell a load of grain, bringing back with him, if he succeeded as he wished, a load of freight for some settlement or town near his home.   There was a great demand for wheat now as many hundreds of emigrants had rushed into the great gold country.   William left the farm to be managed by his prudent little wife and started out on his hundred mile trip.   How little did he dream of the result of this journey!   On his arrival in Sydney after the disposal of his wheat, he walked out to see an old friend named William Andrews who lived in the suburbs of the town.   Here he passed the time until evening when Mr. Andrews remarked, "I say, Chittenden, I've got some brothers come from America, and I am going up to see them. Would you like to go along?"

"Oh, yes," replied William, "I did'nt know you had any brothers in America!"

And so, arm in arm, they entered the little room where several men sat at a table, or pulpit with a strange book in their hands and strange words upon their lips.   Here William heard the sound of the everlasting gospel for the first time.

From the first William felt the truth contained in the words, of the Elders although he knew little or nothing concerning them.

On their way home Mr. Andrews explained to him that these men were his brothers, being brothers in the covenant of Christ.

"And Chittenden," he added, "if any of them go down your way, you'll give them dinner and a bed, won't you, for I know you can?"

"Oh, as to that," replied William, "I would'nt turn a beggar from my door, if he was hungry or wanted a roof to cover him."

William procured a load of freight for a man in Goulburn (one hundred miles further south than Camden) and started on his return trip. His mind was often upon the things he had heard, and he wondered what it all meant. The Elders to whom he had listened were Brothers Farnham, Eldredge, Graham and Fleming, Brother Farnham having charge. They were the second company of Elders ever sent to Australia.

After the departure of William Chittenden, a council was held by the Elders and it was decided that Brothers Fleming and John Eldredge should go up to Camden and the surrounding district. At the last moment however, Elder Fleming was desired to remain in Sydney by Brother Farnham and Elder Graham was sent in his place. I mention this circumstance as it was closely connected with one of Mary's dreams. When William reached his home, he told Mary about these strange men.

"What did you think of them William?"

"Well Mary if they don't speak the truth then I never heard it spoken." And then he went down to Goulburn with his freight.

One lovely day in summer two dusty, tired, hungry men each with a satchel and a walking-cane in their hands, stopped at the wide open door of the Chittenden farm-house. And what saw Mary, when she came to the porch? With a queer throb, she saw in her door the very man who came to her bedside in her dream. She even noticed the low-cut vest showing the white shirt underneath. But as he stepped inside, and her eye fell upon his companion, she saw *he* was not the second one of her dream, although he too carried a cane and satchel. She invited them within, and the first one said,

"We are come, madam, to preach the gospel."

The words, almost identical with those of her dream. Giving her their names, he whose name was Eldredge explained to her that they traveled up from Sydney, and in all the hundred miles, they had found no one willing to give them food and shelter.

Mary bustled around and prepared dinner for her guests. When evening drew near, Brother Eldredge remarked,

"Mrs Chittenden, can you let us remain here over night?"

"Oh," said Mary, "I am afraid I have no place to put you!"

"Well you can let us sit up by your fireside, and that is better than lying on the ground as we have done lately!"

And then Mary assured them that she would do the best she could for them. So a bed was spread out on the floor of the sitting-room, and here the foot-sore Elders were glad to rest their bodies.

The principles and doctrines of these men fell deep into Mary's heart, and like her husband she felt they spoke the truths of heaven.

One evening in conversation with them, Mary told Brother Eldredge that she had seen him before in a dream. But, she added, you were accompanied by another man, not Mr. Graham.

"Ah well, that might have been. You may have seen Brother Fleming for he was coming with me, but Brother Farnham altered the appointments at the last moment!"

And it proved so. When Mary afterwards saw Brother Fleming she recognized him as the second one of her dream.

The Elders were not idle because they had found a comfortable resting place, but traveled about seeking to get opportunities of spreading the gospel One family named Davis, whose farm (rented from McArthur) joined the Chittenden's, listened with pleased interest to these new doctrines. In the course of two weeks after the arrival of the Elders, William Chittenden came home, and expressed a gladness in his heart to find the Elders at his home. He immediately fixed up a bedroom near the sitting-room for the use of the Elders.

Weeks went into months, and still the Chittendens were not baptized.

The Elders made Camden their head-quarters, but went about through the surrounding country, meeting, however, with very little success. William and his wife, with their oldest daughter were ready to be baptized, as were the Davis'. But almost a year after the arrival of the brethren was allowed to slip by without the baptisms having been performed.

I want to stop and tell you a little about the worldly condition of this couple, as well as mention a detail or two more about the country they were living in before I go on with my story.

They had brought their two hundred acres under good cultivation; they had a large fruit garden back of the house, in which grew the most delicious peaches, plums and cherries. The country is so adapted to fruit that peach-stones thrown out near running water would be fruit-bearing-trees in three years. There were no apples, but such quantities of tropical fruits. Grapes, melons, figs, lemons and oranges were so plentiful and so cheap that William would not spend time to grow them. A sixpence (12 cents) would buy enough of these fruits to load a man down.

They had four horses, one wagon, a dray and a light spring cart six cows and many calves, plenty of pigs and droves of chickens, turkeys and geese.

The large granary to the south of the house groaned with its wealth of wheat corn, barley and oats.

And while I am speaking of wheat I am minded to give a description of the way adopted to preserve wheat in that country. Mr. McArthur, the owner of all these thousands of acres, received from his tenants a share of the wheat grown. This he stored up as there was little or no sale for it until drought years, when it commanded a good price.

After the three years drought which occurred there prior to 1853, William and his wife went to this Mr. McArthur to get wheat. He had dug a very large vault or cellar, and this had been well cemented, top, bottom and sides. Here the wheat had been stored for twelve years when the Chittendens went to get theirs. The wheat was perfectly sound and sweet. Over the vault a store-house had been built, and the door to it was near the top of the cellar.

You can see that our kind friends were well-to-do, and had every prospect ahead for success and prosperity.

In the Spring of '54, the Davis family and the Chittendens decided to be baptized. Rumors, and false reports had been rapidly spread about the Latter-day Saints, and their enemies sprang up like magic. Many sarcastic and insulting remarks were made about the "dipping" (as the baptism was called) of the two families. Mr. McArthur was a bitter enemy to the new sect.

One day the Davises were over to Chittenden's and remarked they were going to be baptized the following Monday in the river near their house.

William decided to come over with his family on the same day. So on the 24 of April 1854 William and Mary were baptized by John Eldredge in Camden, Australia. From the moment of their baptism until now no faltering or doubt has ever been in the hearts of these true. Saints. In the evening of the same day, the girls were all baptized by the Elders into the Church of Jesus Christ of Latter-day Saints.

The gospel once having been received the spirit of "gathering" soon follows. And with Mary, who had always wished to go to America, how much more intense that spirit was now!

As she sat and listened to the Elder's description of Zion being built up in the bleak mountains, of the pretty streets lined with shade-trees, and watered by swift-running streamlets she turned to her husband told him that this must be the place of her dream.

William was a very quiet, determined man, who could not be turned from the way he had chosen.

The days, when through the long summer eve-rings, they all sat and listened to the various principles and the new and lovely doctrines unfolded one by one, by the Elders, like the petals of a glorious flower, were the very happiest Mary and her family ever knew. Poor Mary! They were the light which shone over her dreary on-coming future, sometimes brightly, sometimes faintly, but always shining over the wretched, darksome road of the next twenty years.

One little circumstance, which will illustrate Mary's simple but powerful faith will perhaps be worth mentioning and may strengthen some other one's faith. Just before the birth of her eighth girl, which occurred in the Fall after their baptism, she felt low and miserable, scarcely sick enough to be in bed, but too ill to work. One evening Bro. Eldredge was talking to her and said that if she had any sickness or bodily ill, it was her privilege as it was of any member of the Church, to call upon the Elders to administer to her, and then if she exercised faith, it would leave her. Mary had never read a word in her life, and so this came to her as a new and very precious truth.

"Well, Bro. Eldredge, if I can be ministered to and get well, I want to now," said Mary.

So the ordinance was performed, and she was indeed instantly healed. From that day for many months she never felt one moment of illness. And she says to me to-day in her simple quaint way,

"I have never been ministered to in my life since, that I did not get better."

Ever since the arrival of the Elders, the Chittendens had opened their house for them to hold meetings in on Sundays. No other place had ever been obtained, so that the meetings of the Saints, or those who were friendly to them, were still held in Mary's cosy sitting-room.

On the 1st of Nov. 1854, Mary had another daughter whom they named Alice. In two weeks she was up and able to be about the house. The Sunday on which the baby was two weeks old, the family had taken dinner, the things had been washed and set away, and all sat in the dining or sitting-room talking of gathering to Zion.

They had eight girls now, and it would take quite a sum of money to emigrate them all to Utah. So thinking to increase their means a trifle, Mary had taken a little motherless boy, about seven years old, his father paying a certain amount a week for his board. This was money and they would never miss his board as they raised everything which they consumed. This little boy was very troublesome and mischievous. He was very fond of playing out in the hired men's bedroom which was over the granary.

On the Sunday of which I am speaking, he was out in the men's room, and there found some matches. He thought he'd have some rare fun then, so out he ran, matches in hand, and made what he called a "pretty fire," right down close to the pig pens. He watched it burn up, quietly at first, and then —whew!— here is a jolly little breeze catches up the flame, and carries it bravely up right on to the roof of the pig-pen. Then how it did sputter, and crackle, and leap. The boy was old enough to see by that time, that something more than a bit of mischief would grow out of that tiny flame. It spread over the pens like a living thing. Frightened now, he sped away, down to the nearest farm-house, running in and shouting to the gentleman, Mr. Root who lived there, "I didn't set the pig-styes on fire; I struck a match, and it blowed."

Mr. Root hitched up his horse to his water-budge, a cask on wheels which he carried water from a lake near the Chittendens' house, and started on the run for the scene of the boy's wickedness. The Chittendens saw him pass their door running to the lagoon or lake. "I'll declare," said Mary, "is Mr. Root going for water on Sunday? I never knew him to do such a thing before!"

Just then Eliza ran in and said, "Father, the shed is full of smoke."

She had been down to gather eggs from the shed.

The barn, pig-styes, cow sheds, granary, poultry houses and stacks were all at the back of the house and about six rods away.

At last, William got up to go down to the shed to see what was the matter.

When he looked out of the back door, what a sight met his eyes—the whole yard in flames! Others had seen the fire, for the farm-house faced the public-road, and people were all passing there on their road to Chapel. But no one except Mr. Root ever offered a hand of help.

"Oh," said they, " it's those d—d Mormons, let them burn up and go to h——."

The whole family rushed down to the fire and tried to stop its progress but all to no avail. The pigs could not be driven out, and were literally roasted alive. The barn, sheds, pens and every combustible thing went down before the relentless flames. Farm implements of every description, even the grain to the amount of hundreds of bushels, were burned. The flames swept towards the house.

Then how they worked. Everything movable was got out, and the roof was torn off; and the men commenced pouring water on the walls to save them.

"Alas for the rarity of Christian charity." If a few brave men had given help when the fire was first discovered, much might have been saved. But when it was all·over, and Bro. Eldredge and William had thrown themselves on the ground completely exhausted, and the only Christian who had helped them, Mr. Root, had gone home in the same condition, Mary sat out doors with a few of her household goods broken and scattered around her, her two weeks' old babe wailing in her arms, and all that was left of their comfortable home, the empty, blackened, smoking walls of the house looming up in the twilight fast falling around her! Hundreds of cart loads of burnt grain were carted away for the next few days and buried. How many bright hopes and happy plans were buried at the same time, only the future would tell! The roof was speedily put on again, and things inside made as comfortable as might be.

Bro. Eldredge still advised going out to Utah with what means they could scrape up, but William would only shake his head despondently and say, "I dont see how I can do it."

Mary urged all she dared, for she knew the Elders were about to leave for home. It was no use. The only answer she got was, "not now, Mary, not now."

He found an opportunity about that time of going up into the country a hundred miles with some freight. While he was away a gentleman came to the farm-house and wished to buy the good will of the farm.

You will remember William had rented it for twenty-one years. About fourteen years of the lease had expired. The improvements, etc., always went with the lease. So when this gentleman offered to pay three hundred pounds ($1,400) for the remainder of the lease, or the "good-will," as it is termed in that country, Mary thought it a very fortunate thing.

The loss by fire had exceeded three hundred and fifty pounds, or about sixteen or seventeen hundred dollars of our money; and Mary thought if she could sell the lease of the farm, then they could sell what stock and personal property was left them, that making perhaps another two hundred pounds, which might get them all to America. So she sold it; knowing, however, that the bargain would not be legal unless ratified by her husband. She hoped, though, that he would see things as she did. When William reached home Mary told him what she had done.

"Humph; I suppose you know it's of no use unless I give my word, too?"

"Oh, yes," said Mary, sorry to know her husband was so annoyed, "you can, of course, upset it all."

Then she explained all her hopes and plans to him. How they could raise five hundred and fifty pounds, and then they could surely get to America with that tidy sum. "And you know, too, you promised years ago to take me to America."

"And reach there," objected William, "with a big family of little children, and not a shilling to buy 'em bread with. Nice plan, that!"

In vain she argued and plead. William was not to be moved. No one could blame him for not being guided by his wife's advice. Albeit she was a prudent, far-seeing, wise little woman, whose advice had always been proved to be of the best; still the man leads the woman, not woman the man.

But when Brothers Eldredge and Graham counseled him to return with them, it was quite a different matter. They were over him in the Priesthood and had a right to his obedience, even as he exacted obedience from his wife and family. However he still refused, simply saying, "I don't see how I can go just now, Brother Eldredge!"

And so the time passed on, and the Elders left Australia without the Chittendens. The Davis family, who were baptized at the same time as was William and his wife, accompanied the Elders, and part of the same family are now residing in Minersville, Utah.

Here then was the grand mistake of William's life. He did not see it then, nor for years after, but the time came when he wished in the agony of his soul that he had gone to Utah when told to do so, even if he had reached there without one penny to buy a crust of bread on his arrival!

Their girls were all with them and unmarried and
they could have brought their family unbroken to
Utah.   But instead of that twenty-three years
after they came with the merest remnant of their
once large family, leaving almost all their loved
ones behind them, and married to enemies of this
work.

Is not this a grand lesson for our young Elders?
How easy it is to fancy that our own wisdom,
especially about our private affairs, is better than
any one's else! But when the voice of God speaks
through His servants and says, "Do thou so!" woe to
the man who turns from that and works out his own
will in direct opposition.   Let this sink deep into
your hearts, my young readers, and remember
always, God knoweth best!

CHAPTER IV.

ALTHOUGH William was annoyed at the step his
wife had taken, he concluded to let matters go as
they were.   However, much to Mary's chagrin, he
took a farm close by, and tried to make another
start.   Nothing seemed to go right.

On the 24th of July, 1856, Mary gave birth to
another daughter, to whom they gave the name of
Rachel.   The next year another company of
Elders came down from Utah under the leadership

of Brother Stewart. These also made their stopping place, while in that part of the country, at the home of the Chittendens. But if the Elders met with little success during their former mission, this time seemed a complete failure. No one could be found to give them a moment's hearing. One Brother Doudle came up near Camden, and used every endeavor to gain a foot-hold. Instead of kindness he met with cruelty; and in place of bread they threw him a stone. For two days he traveled and could find neither a place to sit down, a crust to eat nor a thing to drink.

When he got back to the Chittendens, he walked wearily in, and Mary's daughter, Jane, bustled around to get him something to eat. "No," said he, "don't cook me a thing. I want nothing but a piece of bread and a drink of water."

She hastily set what he required before him, and after he had eaten he said, "Sister Jane, you shall receive the blessing for this. I have not broken my fast since I left your house until now. I have had to sleep out under the forest trees. I am now fully satisfied there is no place to be had to hold meeting. I thought as I was leaving the city, shall I shake the dust off my feet as a testimony against this people? No, no; I will leave it all in the hands of God!"

The bitter prejudice of people around Camden grew worse and worse. At last the word went out that all the missionaries were to return to Utah immediately. This was in 1857, when Johnson's army was advancing upon Utah,

Before leaving Camden, the Elders prophesied openly that trouble should fall heavily upon the people who had refused them even a hearing. From that time until the "Mormon" missionaries returned and opened the door of mercy, there was not one stalk of grain raised in the whole district of Camden, and people had been unable to obtain a living.

With what earnest prayers did Mary seek to persuade her husband to go along too! And the Elders counseled him to return with them. But no, he could not feel to go with his helpless family and have little or nothing to support them when he arrived in America. So the last Elder bade them good-by and turned away from their door. Alas! eighteen years passed away before they ever heard another Elder's voice.

William was like his wife, unable to read one word, and all that he knew of this gospel had been taught him orally by the missionaries. He was also very young in the faith, and had not learned the great lesson of obedience nor dreamed its mighty weight in this Church. For this reason God was merciful to him, and did not deprive him of the light of the gospel, but taught him the painful but necessary lesson through much and long tribulation. And his children, although scattered and living most of them in Australia, retain the love of the truth in their hearts.

After the Elders had been recalled, Mary commenced to feel a great brooding darkness settle down over her. In the day she could throw it off, but when night closed her labors and laid her at rest, the darkness would fold around her like a garment. She was anything but a nervous, imaginative woman, and this terrible darkness grew into something tangible to her husband as well as to herself. At last he listened to her and decided to once more sell out and get away.

Two more girls were born to Mary before leaving Camden vicinity. One, Caroline, was born May 10, 1858, the other, Louisa, was born June 25, 1860. Mary had then eleven girls, her two sons having died in infancy. The older girls were very much disappointed that neither of the last two were boys. Especially was this the case when Louisa was born; their chagrin being expressed so loudly that it reached their mother's ears. She was a trifle disappointed herself, but when she heard their comments she was really sad and cast down. The feeling could not be shaken off until the next day; when as she lay dozing, a voice plainly said to her: "You shall have a son, and he shall grow up and be a great comfort to you in your old age." As usual she related the circumstance to her husband and he fully believed in it. He thought he would try "sluicing" for gold in some of the mining camps. The process called "sluicing gold," or washing it, is as follows: A box about a foot wide and two feet long, is fitted with several little boards or slats, about an inch high, across the bottom. This is to make the water ripple over. Into this box the sand is shoveled, and the water washes away the dirt leav-

ing tiny nuggets of gold in the bottom of the box.
This is of course in the regions where gold is
found plentifully. Rocks are broken up and shoveled in, and often are richer than the sand. But
this "sluicing" process is a slow one, so much of
the finer portions of gold being washed away. If
quicksilver was used to gather the tiny shining
metal, it would prove much more profitable, but
quicksilver itself is expensive.

So William sold out, and they started up to a
place called Lemon Flat in the early Spring of '61.
All of a sudden severe rains set in ; the country was
flooded, and the soft soil became actually impass-
able. Insomuch so that the family were obliged
to relinquish the idea of going to Lemon Flat and
turned aside to go to another mining camp called
Gunderoo.

While going to Gunderoo the day they reached
the outskirts of the town, was a very tiresome one
for all. Mary had a light, one-seated carriage, a
great deal like the one horse delivery carts in Salt
Lake City. She often got out and walked for exer-
cise. In the latter part of the afternoon, the
wagon, followed by the girls and their father, walking, pushed ahead to reach the summit of the hills
overlooking Gunderoo, or the "gap" as it was
called, there to pitch their tents and prepare
supper.

Mary, walking near the cart, began to feel a
curious weakness creep over her. No pain, only a
weakness in every joint. Alarmed at the long
absence of their mother, two of the oldest girls

hurried back, and found her seated by the road-side unable to proceed another step. They assisted her to rise, and half carried her up the hill to the tents. She whispered to them to put her in bed in the cart where she always slept. They did so. But she grew weaker and weaker. She would faint entirely away, then slowly come back, and wonder feebly what was the matter, and why they all stood around so. Then faint away again, and so on all night. At last Jane remembered her mother had a little consecrated oil packed away, and she searched among the boxes till she found it. They administered to her then, and she revived some. But begged to be taken away from that place.

Her husband felt she might die if he did not comply with her wish, so they started immediately for Yass river. They were traveling along, when Mary's horse gave out. She was obliged then to wait for her husband to return, and get her. She felt much better, and thought she could get out and walk about a little. So she directed the young man who drove her cart to let down the shafts. She got out, but the moment she went to rest her feet on the ground, she fell to the earth. The young man assisted her into the cart again, and then for three months she never stood upon her feet. There was no pain whatever, only an extreme weakness.

While camping on the Yass river the next evening, Mary had a dream which when related sounds like the history of her life for the following twenty years; so true is it in every particular.

She dreamed that she saw herself and her family, traveling, struggling and trying to get a start again. Everything seemed to go against her husband. Sickness came, and she saw herself the only one able to be out of bed. Deadly sickness too, but she was promised that there should be no death. Things seemed to grow blacker and blacker. At last, starvation approached and she saw them all without a morsel of food to eat; everything sold for food, even their clothes. Then when the last remnant of property had been taken from them, the tide turned. She was told they should at last go to Goulburn, where they would break land, and prosperity should once more visit them, and that they should finally reach Zion. The dream was terrible in its reality. She awoke trembling and sobbing, and awaking her husband she told him she had been having a fearful dream.

"I would rather," she added, "have my head severed from my body this minute, than go through what I have dreamed this night."

"Well, wife," answered William, "let us hope it is nothing but a dream."

She related it to him, but he felt too confident in his own strength to believe such a dream as that. It gradually faded from Mary's mind as such things will do, but now and then some circumstance would recall it to her mind with all the vividness of reality.

While camping on the Yass, a stranger came to William and asked him for his daughter Maria, who was then only fourteen years old. William replied that Maria was nothing but a child, and he was an utter stranger, so he could not for a moment think of consenting. Three nights after this, the man stole the girl away, and when morning came and the father discoverd the loss, he was almost frantic with grief. He was a most devoted and affectionate father, and he was fairly beside himself with his daughter's disappearance. He spent money like water. Advertised, went from place to place, searched and hired others to search with him, for the missing girl. It was of no use. She was never found.

While searching for her four of his horses wandered away, and only one ever returned. Then, finally giving up in despair, he hired horses and went to Yass city. Arriving there William obtained work for a man named Gallager, at putting up a barn.

They had been settled but a short time when the baby was prostrated with colonial fever. Mary did all she could, but the child grew worse. Four months went by and still there was no improvement. At last Mary persuaded her husband to get a doctor. The doctor came and told the mother there was one chance in a hundred of the baby's life. No signs of life seemed left in the little body, but he ordered her to put a strong mustard poultice over the stomach. "If it raises a blister," said he, "she will live. If not, she is dead."

Into Mary's mind there suddenly flashed her dream. "Sickness, but no death." Well, then, her baby should live.

A short time after the doctor's departure, Mrs. Gallager, a neighbor, came into the tent, and said, "Mrs. Chittenden, let me hold the child."

"No, Mrs. Gallager, thank you, I would rather hold her."

The woman bustled about and got a tea-kettle of water upon the stove.

"What are you doing," asked Mary.

"Getting a bit of hot water. The child is dead, so we will want some water hot."

"She will not die, Mrs. Gallager. She is going to live."

"Why, woman, she is dead now! Her finger nails are black!"

"No, she is not dead," persisted the mother. Who knows the great power and faith of a mother?

Within a few hours the child's breathing became audible. Her recovery was very slow. And while she still lay weak and ill, William was stricken down by the same complaint. He grew rapidly worse. He too lay ill for several months. He was in a very critical condition, but whenever able to speak he would tell Mary not to bring a doctor, for he should recover without one. The turn for the better came at last, and as soon as he was able to get about a little, they determined to go to Lemon Flat. Their first idea in going to Lemon Flat had been to homestead, or "free select" land, as it is called in Australia. However, they were far too poor now to do this, so William got odd jobs to do. He scraped all he could together, and bought a horse for fifteen pounds. But shortly afterwards, he heard of one of his lost animals about eighteen miles up the country, so he made a trip up to find the animal. Arriving at the place, he heard that a Chinaman had just gone to another camp, on the horse. That night he tethered his horse out, and next morning at daybreak went out as usual for him, and behold, he, too, had disappeared, not leaving a track of a hoof to guide anyone in a search for him. So William was at last obliged to trudge wearily home, eighteen miles, carrying his saddle on his back.

And thus one year dragged heavily by. While here Jane was married to John Carter, and Ellen to a Grecian man named Nicolas Carco. Also, just as they were leaving Lemon Flat, Eliza married a Mr. Griffin.

Now they determined to go once more to Gunderoo to try what could be done there. The reason why William wished to go to Gunderoo was, that no matter what came or went, wages could be made by a man in "sluicing gold." Now the family were almost destitute. After their arrival in Lemon, and for months, most of the children lay sick with the colonial fever.

CHAPTER V.

BETWEEN three or four years had passed since they left Camden (over eight years since the last missionary left Australia), and the Chittendens were much poorer than they were when they left.

For many years Mary had been in the habit of going about to her neighbors, nursing them during confinement. This was a necessity of the country, one woman going to another, as there were no regular nurses to be had. She became acquainted in her labors with a Doctor Haley, the best physician in Goulburn. He always, after the first time when she nursed under him, sent for her. This practice put many an odd pound into her pocket. Her husband was far from idle, however. With his disposition he could never be so. He took charge of the estate of a gentleman named Massy, who was absent in Ireland for eighteen months on business.

As soon as he was released from this situation, where he had earned some money and a good portion of grain, he rented a farm. With anxious hope and honest labor he seeded down twenty acres with the grain he had on hand.

He who sendeth the rains, withholdeth them at His pleasure! For two years there was a complete drouth visited the country. William walked over his field and could not, at the end of the season, pluck one single armful of grain.

While living in this place the promised son was born to Mary, and once again her prophetic dream was realized. He was born May 28, 1865, and William named him Hyrum. When the baby was two years old, little Alice came home from school, and said she felt very sick. As long as there was a second penny in the house, no matter where they were, or what their circumstances, these good parents had kept their children at school. Without education themselves, no effort was spared to give their children the great blessing they had so missed.

Alice came home, quite sick at her stomach, and her mother felt alarmed at once, for her children were regularly and simply fed, and when anything of the kind happened to them she knew it was of an uncommon and serious nature.

Jane had returned to her mother's house, while her husband was up the country on a mining expedition. She had a young baby eleven months old.

When the doctor came next day he pronounced Alice's case one of the most violent scarlet fever. Next day Jane and Rachel came down, and the next day Louisa and Caroline fell ill with the dreadful disease. Jane had the fever so violently that Mary was obliged to wean the baby. Everyone in the family was now ill but herself, and she with a baby two weeks old. For eleven long weeks the anxious mother never had her clothes off, but to change them. The disease was of such a violent type that not one human being had courage or had humanity enough to enter the door. Alone and utterly unaided she went from one bedside to another administering food and medicine. The physician was the only one who ever visited her, and at the times when he came (twice a day) to attend to them, she would sit down long enough to take up her infant and give it the breast.

Three months of sickness, toil and suffering, then the fever spent itself, and Mary could begin to realize their condition financially. Something must be done, for funds were very, very low.

There was a sudden excitement about this time at a place called Mack's Reef, which was three miles from Gunderoo. Gold was found in quartz, and was very rich indeed, at this new camp. William decided to go. So investing their last cent to purchase a simple crushing-mill, and to take themselves out, the Chittendens went to Mack's Reef.

Misfortune was too well acquainted with them now to be driven away, so she curled herself up in the crushing-mill, and behold it failed to do its work. It lost both the gold and the quick-silver.

Matters were now getting desperate. Food was wanted. Strain and economize as she might, Mary could not make things hold out much longer. The pennies followed the shillings, until when the last half-penny had to be taken for flour, William

looked at Mary and said, "Mary, what are we coming to? Must our children starve?"

"No, William, please God! But do you remember my dream? You may not believe it, but I
know it was a true dream. Oh, William, why did
we not go to Zion when we were told? Surely our
sufferings could not be more than they are here.
Here, take these clothes, they are things that I can
spare; you will have to sell them for bread."

And so it went. Garment followed garment,
and yet there seemed no chance of earning a
penny. Finally, there were no more clothes; everything was sold.

Then William took his gun, and went to the
woods. But after a very short time that, too, failed
and they were starving.

That night, when the little children were put
hungry to bed, William walked the floor in the agony
of his mind. "My God!" groaned the wretched man,
"must my children starve before my very eyes?
In my pride I fancied my family would be better
in my hands than in the hands of their Almighty
Father! Oh, that I had listend to counsel!
Now my family are fast leaving my roof, and we
that are left are starving. Starving in a land of
plenty!"

God listened to the prayers of His humbled son,
and he was enabled to get a little something to
eat. But the lesson was not over yet.

Mary had obtained a situation as nurse and this
helped them. William thought he would go up
to Goulburn, a large inland town, where he felt

sure he would find some employment. Accordingly he left the family with Mary, but of course in very wretched circumstances. It was the best that he could do, so Mary was satisfied to be left.

The trip to Goulburn was made in the old spring cart, which had been left of the wreck of their comfortable traveling outfit. The horse, which William had just found previous to starting, was one of the four he had lost on the Yass river. The poor thing had been so abused that it was almost worthless. In fact, it had no money value, for in that country where good stock was comparatively cheap he had tried again and again before leaving Mack's Reef to sell the horse and the cart, or either alone, in order to get flour for his starving family, but no purchaser could be found.

So he went up to Goulburn and took odd jobs as he could get them. When he had been gone some few months, a company of prospecters brought in a new machine to crush the quartz. This fanned the dead embers of hope in every one's breast, and even Mary thought if she could get William to come down and try his quartz in this new mill, they would succeed at last.

But how to get word to him? He was at Goulburn, eighteen miles away. There was no mail, and she had not a vestige of anything to pay for sending word to him. She was very weak too from lack of food. But every one around her was so confident of the grand success about to be made, that she resolved to try to walk up to Goulburn. Accordingly, she set out leaving the baby at home with the girls, and walked feebly towards Goulburn. She was about half-way there when she came to a river. This was forded by teams, but across it had been thrown a plank, and a poor one it was, too. Mary looked at the foaming water, and then at the rotten plank, and felt it would be an impossibility almost to go across. Still, she must get over, so she started; but she had only got a little way out before her head began to reel, she was weak and faint, and about to fall, when she had sense remaining to lay flat down on the plank, and wait for strength. As she prayed for strength and help she heard a horse's hoofs behind her, and a gentleman on horseback dashed into the stream. He rode up to her and said,

"Madam, permit me to help you. Let me take your hand and I will ride close by the board, and thus get you across all right."

"Oh sir, you are very kind," answered Mary as she arose thanking God that He had heard her prayer.

"Where are you going, madam? Pardon me, I do not ask from idle curiosity."

"To Goulburn, sir to my husband."

"I was wondering as I came along, to see a woman on this lonely road. You surely do not expect to reach Goulburn to-night?"

"I thought sir, I would go as far as I could, then lie down and rest until I could go further."

"Well my poor woman, good-by! and success attend you on your journey."

"Many thanks, kind sir, may God reward your kind act." And so he rode on.

Mary went on some distance, and began to feel that she could go no farther. Suddenly she saw a woman approaching her. Wondering, the two women at last met, and the stranger said to Mary,

"Are you the woman a gentleman on horseback assisted across the river?"

"Yes ma'am."

"Then you are to come with me. He has paid us for your supper and lodging to-night. Also, he paid me to come out and meet you and show you the way."

"Thank God! I am almost worn out. What was the gentleman's name, please?"

"That I can't tell. But here's our house. Come, get your supper, it is waiting."

And thus was her humble prayer answered, and a friend raised up to her in her sore need.

The next day Mary reached Goulburn, and she and her husband returned the following day in the cart, to Mack's Reef. But after reaching the Reef, William found it would require quite a sum of money to do anything with his quartz, so at last abandoning everything, he left the Reef in disgust. The poor old horse died shortly after that, and thus they only had the cart remaining. The harvest time was approaching, and William had the rent to pay on the farm he had taken, and which had failed so dismally. So he went to the owner and offered to harvest out the amount. The offer was accepted, and he went harvesting the remainder of the season.

Meantime, Mary had been sent for, to nurse a lady who lived a few miles out from Gunderoo. So, not liking to lose so good an opportunity of making a bit of money, she weaned her ten month's old baby, and left him at home with the girls. She was engaged for a month, receiving a pound a week, about twenty dollars a month, for her services.

.When she returned, she found her husband at home. You know, William, I told you my dream would surely be fulfilled. Are you not willing to. admit that so far it has come true every word?"

"Well yes, Mary, but what then?"

"Then, in my dream we were to lose everything before the turn would come, and we should commence to prosper. We've nothing left now but the spring cart. Give that, as it is too poor to sell, to Isaac Norris. Then let us go to Goulburn, and once more try farming. You know we must break land there."

"Thou art like a woman. If we part with the cart, how, pray, shall we get to Goulburn." "Why, William, have I not brought home four pounds? That will move us to Goulburn. Come husband, let us get away from here." At length William consented; the spring cart was given to their son-in-law, Isaac Norris, and the whole family moved up to Goulburn. Their daughter Alice was soon after married to a Mr. Larkum, and had one child named Lavinia by him. The girl was treated very badly, and at last gave the child to her mother to raise. Mary has never since been separated from this child, but has reared her as her own. Four or five years passed away, William farming and Mary nursing at times. William did the farming for a widow lady named Day, who kept a lodging-house about four miles out from Goulburn. She was a very fine, active, kind-hearted woman, and for the next ten years, was a true friend to the Chittendens. In fact, the best friend they ever had in Australia. Mary used often to go up to her house, when not out nursing, for a week at a time to assist the widow with her work. Goulburn is a very large, handsome, inland town in Australia, situated in the midst of a rich farming district. On one side of the town, away to the left, was a large hill, covered with fine timber. The Chittendens had rented a small house about four miles out from Goulburn.

About five years after their coming to Goulburn, Mary had another dream. A personage came to her and began talking to her of her affairs. This personage said to her among other things:

"You shall take a farm, on the opposite side of the road to where you now live. And, after, you shall prosper exceedingly. Then you shall take money, constantly, from this side of the road, and you shall be blessed, insomuch that you shall soon go to Zion thereafter." When she awoke, she told the dream to her husband. Shortly after this a rumor reached them that a certain man named Grimson was about to give up his farm, which he rented from a gentleman named Gibson. This surely must be the place of her dream, for was it not across the road from them? And so she talked to her husband about the matter. But he had no sympathy nor hope to give her on the subject.

"Mary how can you think of such a thing? What could I do with a farm? I haven't a tool nor an animal to use. It is impossible. So don't talk of it."

But Mary was far from satisfied. However, she knew her husband too well to urge the matter, when he spoke as he had done. And further, in a very short time after the farm was vacated, it was re-let to another person. Mary was thus forced to give it up. A month or so slipped by, and one night Mary dreamed the same dream, in relation to the farm across the road. She thought, however, she would not mention it to her husband. In a week or so, they again heard the farm was to let, as the family was dissatisfied. Then Mary made bold to tell her husband of the repetition of the dream, and beg him to try and take it.

"Why do you keep urging me about that farm, Mary? I have not one thing to do with. I tell you it is impossible."

And again disappointed, Mary thought she would say no more about the matter. That day she was going up to spend a week at Mrs. Day's assisting her in her housework and cleaning. After she arrived there, she prepared breakfast, and she and Mrs. Day sat down to eat. As they were talking, Mrs. Day said, "Why doesn't Mr. Chittenden take that farm of Gibson's? I hear it is again vacant. He is a good farmer, and could easily attend to that as well as look after mine."

"He would like to do so, no doubt, but he thinks he could not on account of having nothing to do with, no teams nor machines, nor in fact anything."

"Well, if that's where the trouble lies, I'll tell you what I'll do. He shall have the use of my horses and plows and all the farm machines for nothing, and I will furnish him seed grain for the first year, and he can let me have it back after he gets a start."

"Oh Mrs. Day, you are too good to us."

"Not a bit of it. I would do more than that to keep you in the country. You know that I could not possibly live without your help," replied the lady, laughingly.

Mary could hardly contain herself for joy. And when night came, she begged to be allowed to go home that night, as she could not wait a whole week before telling her husband the good news.

Accordingly she hurried home that night and told her husband what Mrs. Day had said.

"Mary," said William, "if Mrs. Day tells me the same as she tells you, I'll take Gibson's farm."

So early the next morning they started on their errand. The farm house opposite them was vacant, and as they passed Mary asked herself, tremblingly, if they should be sufficiently blessed to live there. Mrs. Day greeted them very kindly and told them they were just in time for breakfast.

"Thank you, Mrs. Day; but Mary has been telling me you spoke to her about our taking Gibson's farm."

"So I did, Chittenden; and I tell you if you'll take the farm, keeping mine too, mind, you shall have the use of my team, wagon and farm implements. Besides, I will lend you your seed grain for the first year, and you can return it afterwards."

"Well, Mrs. Day, if you are so kind as that, all I can do is to thank you and accept the offer. I will go right on to Mr. Gibson at once and make the bargain."

Mr. Gibson was quite pleased to have William take the farm. That same week the family moved across the road, and Mary felt like a new woman.

During all these fifteen years you may be sure Mary and William had often talked of the religion that was so dear to both. Their daughters, although they had, perforce, married those outside the Church, were staunch "Mormons," and are to this day.

One day William met Mr. Gibson who said, "I have been thinking, William, you can open a gate on the other side of the road, opposite your own door, and make a bit of a road to the woods, and you can take toll from the gate. You know you live on the public turnpike from Goulburn, and this toll road would be a good thing to the Goulburn people."

"How much could you allow me, sir?"

"Five shillings from every pound. Then your children could attend the gate."

Very well, I will do so, and am very grateful to you for the privilege."

"Well, mother," said William soon after, as he entered the house, "your money is coming from the other side of the road."

And when he had laughingly told her how, she said she felt more like crying than laughing, she was so grateful to God.

CHAPTER VI.

THE story of prosperity is so much easier to tell, and in truth is so much shorter than the tale of adversity and suffering, that we may well hasten over the remaining five years of their waiting in that far-distant land.

Everything prospered. But about the second year William's health commenced to break down. Gradually he became more and more incapable of work, until at last, one day, he came in and throwing himself down, he exclaimed, "Mary, I have done my last day's work." It was even so. But God did not fail them.

In 1875, two men came up to the door, and asked for food and shelter. When they announced themselves as Elders from Utah, Mary's hands were outstretched and her heart filled with great joy, even as her eyes ran over with happy tears.

The Elders were Jacob Miller of Farmington, and David Cluff of Provo, since dead. A month or two afterwards, Elder Charles Burton and John M. Young of Salt Lake City, also were warmly welcomed at the farm.

William's illness was Bright's disease of the kidneys, and he was slowly dying.

They left Sydney on the 7th of April, 1877, for Utah, six souls in all, William and Mary, their children Caroline, Louise and Hyrum, with the one grandchild, Lavinia.

On their arrival they went at once to Provo. William had much more to bear of poverty and suffering, than any one could have dreamed, even after their arrival here. Mary went out washing to eke out their store, (they had barely ten dollars left,) and the two girls got positions in the factory.

Within a year, Caroline married Eleazer Jones, and Louisa married Abraham Wild. The last named couple live near their mother now.

Caroline has moved with her husband to Arizona. Mary's eldest daughter, Mary Ann Mayberry, also came with her husband and family to Utah in 1879.

I would not linger if I could on the severe suffering, and painful death of William, just twelve month from the day they left home.

When the sad day came on which he left them all, in spite of his awful agony, he called his only boy Hyrum, who was then thirteen years old, and stretching out the thin, wasted hands he blessed him fervently, and said, "You are going to be a good boy to your mother, I think?"

"Yes, father, I will," answered the lad, manfully.

"My boy, I can do nothing, no work in the Temple for her, nor for myself; I have got to go."

"If you have got to go, father," tremblingly said the boy, "I will do all that lies in my power."

"Remember mother, Hyrum, she has been good to us, and worked hard for us all her days." Then again he blessed him, and soon the peaceful end came, and the poor aching frame was at rest.

A year or two of hard, constant work at the wash tub passed away, and one night the personage who had visited Mary before came to her in a dream and said:

"Mary, the time has now come for you to go and do the work for yourself and your husband. If you will go, you shall soon have a home afterwards."

Here was a command and a promise. Hyrum had shot up and was a tall, quiet-mannered young man, and had gone out on a surveying expedition, carrying chains for the men, to earn some money. His great ambition was to get a home for his mother.

On his return from the surveying expedition he put nearly $100.00 into his mother's hands. A day or two after he said, "Mother I would like to go down to St. George and do father's work; you know I promised him to do it as soon as I could, and this is the first money I have ever had. I am sixteen years old, and if the Bishop thinks I am worthy, I would like to go."

Mary quickly told her dream, which she had hesitated mentioning, fearing he would not like it, but he believed it.

"Mother, I will go this very night," he said when she had concluded her story, "and see what the Bishop says."

So down he went, and Bishop Booth very willingly told him to go, and he felt pleased to give the necessary recommends.

They went and had a most glorious time, and on her return Mary went to washing again. But mark! In less than one year from that time they had bargained for a place, and got two little rooms built upon it.

If you come to Provo, go and see dear old Sister Chittenden; she is sixty-six years old, and quite a hearty, happy little woman yet.

She meditatively pushes aside her neat, black lace cap from her ear, with her finger, as I ask what to say to you in farewell, and with mild but tearful eyes, says:

Tell them for me, always to be obedient to the counsel of those who are over them; and obey the whisperings of God, trusting to Him for the result! And then, God bless them all! Amen."

A HEROINE OF HAUN'S MILL MASSACRE.

THE name of Sister Amanda, or Mrs. Warren Smith, is well known to the Latter-day Saints. She has had a most eventful life, and the terrible tragedy of Haun's Mill, in Caldwell county, when her husband and son were killed, and another son wounded, have made her name familiar to all who have read the history of the mobbings and drivings in the State of Missouri. Mrs. Smith was born in Becket, Birkshire Co., Mass., Feb. 22, 1809. Her parents were Ezekiel and Fanny Barnes; she was one of a family of ten children. Her grandfather, on her mother's side, James Johnson, came from Scotland in an early day, and in the revolutionary war held the office of general; he was a great and brave man. Sister Smith says that her father left Massachusetts when she was quite young and went up to Ohio, and settled in Amherst, Lorain county, where the family endured all the privations and hardships incident to a new country. The following is her own narrative:

"At eighteen years of age I was married to Warren Smith; we had plenty of this world's goods and lived comfortable and happily together, nothing of particular interest transpiring until Sidney Rigdon and Orson Hyde came to our neigh-

borhood preaching Campbellism. I was converted
and baptized by Sidney Rigdon; my husband did
not like it, yet gave his permission. I was at that
time the mother of two children. Soon after my
conversion ·to the Campbellite faith, Simeon D.
Carter came preaching the everlasting gospel, and
on the 1st day of April, 1831, he baptized me into
the Church of Jesus Christ of Latter-day Saints,
of which I have ever since been a member. My
husband was baptized shortly after and we were
united in our faith.

"We sold out our property in Amherst and went
to Kirtland, and bought a place west of the Temple,
on the Chagrin river, where we enjoyed ourselves
in the society of the Saints, but after the failure of
the Kirtland bank and other troubles in that place,
in consequence of our enemies, we lost all our property except enough to fit up teams, etc., to take
us to Missouri. We started in the Spring of 1838,
and bade farewell to the land of our fathers and
our home to go and dwell with the Saints in what
then seemed a far-off place.

"There were several families of us and we traveled on without much difficulty until we came to
Caldwell county, Missouri. One day as we were
going on as usual, minding our own business, we
were stopped by a mob of armed men, who told us
if we went another step they would kill us all. They
commenced plundering, taking our guns from our
wagons, which we had brought, as we were going
into a new country, and after thus robbing us took
us back five miles, placed a guard around us, and

kept us there in that way three days, and then let us go. We journeyed on ten miles further, though our hearts were heavy and we knew not what might happen next. Then we arrived at a little town of about eight or ten houses, a grist and saw mill belonging to the Saints. We stopped there to camp for the night. A little before sunset a mob of three hundred armed men came upon us. Our brethren halloed for the women and children to run for the woods, while they (the men) ran into an old blacksmith shop.

"They feared, if men, women and children were in one place, the mob would rush upon them and kill them all together. The mob fired before the women had time to start from the camp. The men took off their hats and swung them and cried for quarter, until they were shot down; the mob paid no attention to their entreaties, but fired alternately. I took my little girls (my boys I could not find) and ran for the woods. The mob encircled us on all sides, excepting the bank of the creek, so I ran down the bank and crossed the mill pond on a plank, ran up the hill on the other side into the bushes; and the bullets whistled by me like hailstones, and cut down the bushes on all sides of me. One girl was wounded by my side, and she fell over a log; her clothes happened to hang over the log in sight of the mob, and they fired at them, supposing that it was her body, and after all was still our people cut out of that log twenty bullets.

"When the mob had done firing they began to howl, and one would have thought a horde of demons had escaped from the lower regions. They plundered our goods, what we had left, they took possession of our horses and wagons, and drove away, howling like so many demons. After they had gone I came down to behold the awful scene of slaughter, and, oh! what a horrible sight! My husband and one of my sons, ten years old, lay lifeless upon the ground, and another son, six years old, wounded and bleeding, his hip all shot to pieces; and the ground all around was covered with the dead and dying. Three little boys had crept under the blacksmith's bellows; one of them received three wounds; he lived three weeks, suffering all the time incessantly, and at last died. He was not mine, the other two were mine. One of whom had his brains all shot out, the other his hip shot to pieces." This last was Alma Smith, who lives at Coalville, and who still carries the bullets of the mob in his body, but was healed by the power of God through the careful nursing and earnest faith of his mother. "My husband was nearly stripped of his clothes before he was quite dead; he had on a new pair of calf-skin boots, and they were taken off him by one whom they designated as Bill Mann, who afterward made his brags that he 'pulled a d—d Mormon's boots off his feet while he was kicking.' It was at sunset when the mob left and we crawled back to see and comprehend the extent of our misery. The very dogs seemed filled with rage, howling over their dead masters, and the cattle caught the scent of innocent blood, and bellowed. A dozen helpless widows grieving for the loss of their husbands, and thirty or forty orphaned or fatherless children were screaming and crying for their fathers, who lay cold and insensible around them. The groans of the wounded and dying rent the air. All this combined was enough to melt the heart of anything but a Missouri mobocrat. There were fifteen killed and ten wounded, two of whom died the next day."

"As I returned from the woods, where I had fled for safety, to the scene of slaughter, I found the sister who started with me lying in a pool of blood. She had fainted, but was only shot through the hand. Further on was Father McBride, an aged, white-haired revolutionary soldier; his murderer had literally cut him to pieces with an old corn-cutter. His hands had been split down when he raised them in supplication for mercy. Then one of the mob cleft open his head with the same weapon, and the veteran who had fought for the freedom of his country in the glorious days of the past, was numbered with the martyrs. My eldest son, Willard, took my wounded boy upon his back and bore him to our tent. The entire hip bone, joint and all were shot away. We laid little Alma upon our bed and examined the wound. I was among the dead and dying; I knew not what to do. I was there all that long dreadful night with my dead and my wounded, and none but God as physician and help. I knew not but at any moment the mob might return to complete their dreadful work. In the extremity of my agony I cried unto the Lord, 'O, Thou who hearest the prayers of the widow and fatherless, what shall I do? Thou knowest my inexperience, Thou seest my poor, wounded boy, what shall I do? Heavenly Father, direct me!' And I was directed as if by a voice speaking to me. Our fire was smouldering; we had been burning the shaggy bark of hickory logs. The voice told me to take those ashes and make a solution, then saturate a cloth with it and put it right into the wound. It was painful, but my little boy was too near dead to heed the pain much. Again and again I saturated the cloth and put it into the hole from which the hip joint had been plowed out, and each time mashed flesh and splinters of bone came away with the cloth, and the wound became white and clean. I had obeyed the voice that directed me, and having done this, prayed again to the Lord to be instructed further; and was answered as distinctly as though a physician had been standing by·speaking to me. A slippery elm tree was near by, and I was told to make a poultice of the roots of the slippery elm and fill the wound with it. My boy Willard procured the slippery elm from the roots of the tree; I made the poultice and applied it. The wound was so large it took a quarter of a yard of linen to cover it. After I had properly dressed the wound, I found vent to my feelings in tears for the first time, and resigned myself to the anguish of the hour. All through the night I heard the groans of the sufferers, and once in the dark we groped our way over the heap of dead in the blacksmith shop, to try to soothe the wants of those who had been mortally wounded, and who lay so helpless among the slain.

"Next morning Brother Joseph Young came to the scene of bloodshed and massacre. 'What shall be done with the dead?' he asked. There was no time to bury them, the mob was coming on us; there were no men left to dig the graves. 'Do anything, Brother Joseph,' I said, 'except to leave their bodies to the fiends who have killed them.' Close by was a deep, dry well. Into this the bodies were hurried, sixteen or seventeen in number. No burial service, no customary rites could be performed. All were thrown into the well except my murdered boy, Sardius. When Brother Young was assisting to carry him on a board to the well, he laid down the corpse and declared he could not throw that boy into the horrible, dark, cold grave. He could not perform the last office for one so young and interesting, who had been so foully murdered, and so my martyred son was left unburied. 'Oh, they have left my Sardius unburied in the sun,' I cried, and ran and covered his body with a sheet. He lay there until the next day, and then I, his own mother, horrible to relate, assisted by his elder brother, Willard, went back and threw him into this rude vault with the others, and covered them as well as we could with straw and earth.

"After disposing of the dead the best that we could, we commended their bodies to God and felt that He would take care of them, and of those whose lives were spared. I had plenty to do to take care of my little orphaned children, and could not stop to think or dwell upon the awful occurrence. My poor, wounded boy demanded constant care, and for three months I never left him night or day. The next day the mob came back and told us we must leave the State, or they would kill us all. It was cold weather; they had taken away our horses and robbed us of our clothing; the men who had survived the massacre were wounded; our people in other parts of the State were passing through similar persecutions, and we knew not what to do.

"I told them they might kill me and my children in welcome. They sent to us messages from time to time, that if we did not leave the State they would come and make a breakfast of us. We sisters used to have little prayer meetings, and we had mighty faith; the power of God was manifested in the healing of the sick and wounded. The mob told us we must stop these meetings, if we did not they would kill every man, woman and child. We were quiet and did not trouble anyone. We got our own wood, we did our own milling, but in spite of all our efforts to be at peace, they would not allow us to remain in the State of Missouri. I arranged everything, fixed up my poor, wounded boy, and on the first day of February started, without any money, on my journey towards the State of Illinois; I drove my own team and slept out of doors. I had four small children, and we suffered much from cold, hunger and fatigue.

"I once asked one of the mob what they intended when they came upon our camp; he answered they intended to 'kill everything that breathed.' I felt the loss of my husband greatly, but rejoiced that he died a martyr to the cause of truth. He went full of faith and in hope of a glorious resurrection. As for myself I had unshaken confidence in God through it all.

"In the year 1839 I married again, to a man bearing the same name as my deceased husband (Warren Smith), though they were not in the least related. He was also a blacksmith and our circumstances were prosperous. By this marriage I had three children, Amanda Malvina, who died in Nauvoo; also Warren Barnes and Sarah Marinda, who are still living, the former at American Fork and is counselor to the Bishop, the latter at Hyde Park.

"I enjoyed the privilege of seeing the Temple finished, and of receiving therein the blessing of holy ordinances. Willard, my first-born son, also had his endowments in that Temple, and came out among the first who left there; was one of the Mormon Battalion, who were called to go to Mexico while we were *en route* to find a resting place for the Saints. Willard is now, and has been for several years past, President of Morgan Stake."

During the time they lived in Nauvoo, President Joseph organized a Relief Society. Sister Smith became a member of its first organization and greatly rejoiced in the benevolent work; much good was accomplished by it.

In July, 1847, they started from Nauvoo intending to go with the Saints to the Rocky Mountains, but for the want of sufficient means for so long a journey they were compelled to stop in Iowa. They remained until the year 1850, when they took up their line of march for Salt Lake City, arriving on the 18th of September, safe and well. Shortly after arriving in this city, her husband, who had been for some time dilatory in his duties, apostatized from the faith, and they separated. She took the children with her and provided for herself.

On the 24th of January, 1854, a number of ladies met together to consider the importance of organizing a society for the purpose of making clothes for the Indians and other charitable work, which was properly organized Feb. 9th. Sister Smith was one of the officers of the society, which resulted in much temporal good being accomplished.

In consequence of the many hardships she endured through the persecutions in Missouri which were heaped upon her and her family by a relentless mob, her health was undermined, and as years increased, infirmities settled upon her which rendered her unable to retain the position she had held in the Relief Society. She was honorably released and will ever be remembered by the Bishop and his counselors and the members of the Ward for her benevolence and self-denial in ministering to the unfortunate.

Sister Smith has much to rejoice over even in her present affliction, for she has raised her family in the principles of the gospel of Christ and the fear of God, and they remain true and steadfast to the faith of the latter-day work. A good woman, who has reared to manhood and womanhood a large family almost without a father's help, is certainly worthy of commendation and must have great satisfaction in her life and labor. She has been for more than fifty years a member of the Church of Jesus Christ of Latter-day Saints.

There are very few now living who have a record of more than half a century in the Church. Sister Smith has endeared herself to a very large number of the Latter-day Saints, who are ever ready to do her honor for her faith, integrity and the many estimable qualities which have beautified and adorned her life.

Her testimony of the massacre at Haun's mill, in Missouri, is that of an eye witness and participator. Indeed she might with all propriety be termed the heroine of that fearful tragedy, for her sublimity of courage surpassed that of ordinary mortals. God was with her in His power in her hour of severe trouble and she was indeed a host in herself. In conclusion we would say, may heaven's choicest blessings rest upon her the remainder of her days here upon the earth, and her heart be filled with joy and peace continually and may she continue to bear a faithful testimony to the truth, and live until she has accomplished all she has ever anticipated for the living and the dead.   E. B. W.

www.ingramcontent.com/pod-product-compliance
Lightning Source LLC
Chambersburg PA
CBHW020038030726
47499CB00007B/2479